How To Bring Him Back

Claire HM

First published October 2021 by Fly on the Wall Press

Published in the UK by Fly on the Wall Press

56 High Lea Rd

New Mills

Derbyshire

SK22 3DP

www.flyonthewallpress.co.uk

Copyright Claire HM © 2021

ISBN: 9781913211479

Supported using public funding by

ARTS COUNCIL ENGLAND

LOTTERY FUNDED

For our little group that's always been.

1.

March 2018

If I was going to cast a spell tonight, this night of a full arse moon, stark as a ten-day crust of snow, I'd start by telling the earth to spin in the opposite direction.

By what power?

By the power of my pen.

Not some scratchy biro, but this big-barrelled fountain pen, that knocks back ink like the first pint of the evening. Because I know that time, and its bloody mouth can suck in that big gut of yours, Stadd. Because I know my pen can pump back brown into your greying hair.

The spinning of the earth whips you into your superhero costume - cherry DMs and your old Crombie coat. And by the power of my swaggering pen that counter-spinning drags you, I draw you, ten thousand miles and twenty years back to me.

And why would I want to cast this spell?

So I can start my apology.

December 1994

Cait's been sitting on the floor of the bus shelter for an hour, and her arse feels as bitter and hard as the slabs underneath it. Stadd hasn't been able to drag her onto any of the buses that have turned up since she's been slumped here. But now, finally, her head is numb too. Turns out the cold wipes out indecision better than vodka.

She isn't going to move.

A bus will only take her home. What's that old bullshit proverb about hearts and homes? Well her heart's so stuffed with shit, how is it even finding contraction enough to beat?

She watches Stadd lean his face towards the bus shelter wall, one hand spread on the timetable, the other still inside the pocket of his Crombie. She presses her cheek on the sleeve of her leather jacket. It's raw with the cold air. Leather jackets – keep you sweaty in June, and glacial in December. What exactly is the fucking point of them?

Stadd turns to her, squeezes his shoulders to his ears, shudders.

"That was definitely the last bus, you know. We'll have to get a cab."

Yeah, she can do that. He doesn't know her address so that's safe. She won't end up at home. She nods, lets him slide his hands underneath the armpits of her leather and hoist her up. Cait can make eight stone two very heavy indeed.

In the back of the cab, Stadd brushes off the rain from

6

his coat, rubs his glasses with his scarf, wraps his arm around Cait. Even through her jacket, his hand is warm.

"Where to, mate?" asks the driver.

Stadd bows his face to Cait, and she tries to fix her eyes on the rim of condensation around his lenses. He gives directions to the driver, to his house. She turns her head towards the window. There's no reason for her to break the silence yet.

The driver doesn't feel the same way.

"Been somewhere nice?"

"At the Ice Palace," Stadd replies.

"Good in there, is it?"

Perhaps the driver is imagining the latest bar, what with nothing in Stadd's flat delivery bearing any of the markers of a joke.

"No, mate, it was fucking freezing. Any chance of turning up your blowers?"

It's hard for Cait to make sense of what she can see – red light smeared across puddles, a haze of metal, road signs that go by so fast she doesn't have time to see where she is. The only thing she can make out for sure is that it's still pissing down.

She tries to remember when Rik left the pub tonight, if he'd noticed how long she was talking to Stadd, if he'd stayed long enough to see the kiss. Had Rik punched another wall, or would the fact that Stadd was his mate make it less likely for Rik to kick off?

As the taxi slows down, Cait knows from the streak of double fronted houses that Stadd lives with his parents. So she isn't the only fucking loser around here. Stadd gives a couple of notes to the driver with his free hand and then turns back to her.

"We need to get out here."

He shuffles along the backseat, keeping Cait tight to him, dragging her a little at a time until he gets to the cab door. She's a sealed-up box, marked fragile, contents unknown, being edged across the seat.

"I'm opening the door now, Cait, don't fall out."

It turns out the driver was not oblivious to her state.

"Are you sure she's not going to vom? That's a fifty quid surcharge."

"We're fine here, just give us another minute. And keep the change."

Stadd is standing outside the cab now, his hands wrapped around the fists Cait makes. Her head bows forward, hair caught between her lips. She wants to speak, but isn't sure if Stadd will understand, her mouth oozing with saliva.

"Carry me."

"That's not happening. Lean into me as you stand up."

It's good to know how far he'll go, where his limits lie.

Stadd leads Cait through the doorway, a flowery disinfectant smell smothering her nostrils. Her breathing shallows out to avoid a vomit situation. She tries to lean into him less but her head, her hip, the whole side of her leg all just slump more.

8

In the hallway there is a row of framed blurry pictures of many, many children. But maybe they are the same child? She struggles to focus on the picture closest to her. The gold wire of the child's glasses dances within the frame.

"We're nearly in the back room. A couple of steps. Mind the door frame."

"I need to lie down."

"Just lie on the carpet now while I set up the bed."

Stadd kneels and Cait lets him take more of her weight as she tumbles against him. The flowery stench is less intense in this room so she deepens her breathing again. Then, with one hand on her back and the other pressed into the wire of her bra, Stadd lowers her to the floor.

She lies there as he rolls her onto her side, arranges her so she can feel the curve of her body making a 'C' shape, legs dangling down to form the tail of a question mark. Warm fingertips stroke her fringe.

"Hey, don't go to sleep just yet."

The last thing Cait remembers is Stadd insisting she open her eyes, but the warmth and the vodka, at last, demolish her.

* * *

Cait wakes up face down in a pillow, hair wet against her open mouth, tasting of sweat and her stale tongue. It's hard to move in the dried-out stiffness of her ripped jeans, her bloated stomach garrotted by the waistband. She has to press both palms into the soft surface beneath her, then flip herself over like a burger. Which does not do the spinning head any good. Or that pounding behind her right eye. She uses her

9

good eye to scan the unfamiliar surroundings. Curved back chairs, matching table and a glass-fronted cabinet of crockery - even with her right eye scrunched shut Cait can see enough to know that she's been put up in the dining room.

Who's dining room?

Right, yeah, Stadd's.

But what about Rik?

No, the pounding in her head's too sickening. Can't think about that yet.

It feels like the night has been one long blink. One long, restless blink, punctuated by that same dream she's had since the last year of juniors. The man who lives on top of a cupboard and chases her with a knife, a tuft of bush poking out above his y-fronts. But it has to have been more than a blink. The light streams through the side of long curtains at her feet and tells her it's already deep into the morning.

Perhaps Stadd has been waiting outside, perhaps it's just coincidental timing, but as the sofa bed creaks with the strain of Cait pulling herself up into a sitting position she hears the rustle of the door behind her being pushed open over thick carpet. She whips her head round and immediately regrets the sudden movement.

Stadd's face swims in a constellation of visual disturbance. Cait can't make out which speckles of matter belong to his face and which belong to the dining room wall.

"So you are alive," he says.

She swallows the wateriness that has started to gather in her mouth again, waiting until the edge between Stadd's face and the chintzy wallpaper forms a clear line.

"Sadly, very sadly."

Stadd shuts the door behind him and makes his way to sit on the edge of the sofa bed. He's dressed in jeans and a thick cabled cardigan. His hair is already quiffed, but he has a patchy shadow of stubble on his cheeks that he squeezes between his thumb and middle finger as he replies to her.

"Until you're up and moving there's no evidence for that."

Cait is hoping that the light is hazy enough in the room to paint her face into soft focus. Then she starts to panic that she has no fucking idea what her hair is doing. Since she'd bleached it, her hair's been unpredictable even in kinder circumstances. Like ones with conditioner, hairspray, a brush.

"For that to happen I'm going to need milky coffee. Strong. No sugar."

'Toast?'

"I don't do breakfast. Have you got work today?"

"No, strictly weekday shifts for me. Anything else encroaches too much on drinking time."

Stadd looks tired but basically himself. There's no awkwardness between them. She doesn't get the sense he's trying to get rid of her. Not like Rik. Rik in the morning was always rough as fuck, the dark curtains of his hair scrunched into a bird's nest on whatever side he had passed out on, never taking the time to smooth it down in the rush to get her out of the door.

"Stadd?"

"Yeah?"

"Are your Mom and Dad about?"

"Yeah. And they can't wait to see what the hell I've dragged home."

Cait groans and flops her face down onto the duvet. Whatever just hiccupped into her mouth she swallows straight back down. Pull it together, Cait. Stadd is a decent guy. Here's a chance to leave Rik and the chasing and the lying and all that chaos behind. Stop being such a fuck up. Don't make being a fuck up an actual choice.

"Until I get to the mirror, I won't be sure myself."

March 2018

I've done it, Stadd. I've cast the spell and I've started to bring you back, back to this empty beach. Sitting on this rock. Torch at my feet. Wind whipping around my face. My hand cramping into a claw as I slowly freeze off my lady balls. I've broken through time.

Ten years ago, back when Facebook was all shiny excitement and worth bothering with to see who'd hunt you out, you messaged me. The picture on your profile showed you hadn't changed much: your dark quiff had been cropped, but you still had glasses Morrissey would be proud of. The thing was, you messaged me with the strangest opening line.

I don't know if you remember me but...

You didn't know if I remembered you?

I remember afternoon drinking, evening drinking, bus stops, taxis. I remember soft kisses from brow to neck, hands holding the weight of my head.

I remember you and Rik and my dog shit choices. I remember crying on a lumpy bedsit mattress, each hangover blacker than the next.

I remember turning into a monster.

Monstress.

You told me about your new life in Oz, as far as you could get from the shit of Birmingham. Your heart following a sheila called Sooz. It dawned on me then what a soppy fuck you'd been. A soppy fuck caught off guard with a jagged stab in the dick. Me at twenty-one. I've never treated anybody as badly as I treated you.

Tomorrow, I'm forty-five. The bulge of my muffin top suggests my relationship to food has tipped a little too far in the direction of comfort. But I'm happy with that. Happy enough. My hair's still dark at the roots. In hazy light I sometimes get eyeballed.

But how fucking old did you get?

I dreamt about you last week. It was just a dream about a kiss, but as I stood in front of you I felt so strong and grounded, it was like my feet had grown roots. And when I looked down, they had. Straw-coloured tendrils were sprouting from my feet into crumbly black soil. They swirled and intertwined with the thick green roots curling from the ridges of your *AirWair* soles.

All the next day my mind was filled with the dream. I felt like I'd missed a truth about you that would tell me something I still need to find out about myself. I knew if I spent time with my memories at the least I'd get a story to write about you, about us.

I'd long since deleted my Facebook account so I had to search deeper this time to find your face. Perhaps you still lived in the same place in Oz? You did. Your name, your state and Google images. It's all I needed. I nearly scrolled past that black and white thumbnail.

Twenty years has a sicker sense of humour than ten.

You weren't the man who knew me knew me after I poured myself back from that coastal university. Where was your hair? What was that hairline? Was that a sports collar beneath your bulging chin? You weren't the man who'd chased a dropout, a failure. Fuck, I was shattered back then: not tired but broken. Broken in a way that I thought I could never put myself back together again.

So I didn't try to.

Instead, I learnt that men as different as you and Rik could still be attracted to a broken glass woman, a makeshift shiv pointing straight at the groin.

The full moon is tarting it up with a single strip of cloud, and my lady balls have had all the freezing they can take for tonight. It's time to gather up tools and go back to the room; listen to these waves crashing through the single glazing as it drags me into sleep.

2.

March 2018

I can't stay asleep in this haunted room.

The ghost staggers with her brassy hair, dark at the roots. Her lips are still fat and the colour of smashed cherries. Powder cakes around her open pores. Bones poke above a scant cami top. But, Jesus, her eyes. They're just hungry holes, sucking it all up. She cannot choose: she wants to be with everyone. She wants to be everyone. She wants to take over me, slip into me, use my tongue to slur her words.

You know it, Stadd. You were the one conjured here but she is the dybbuk, the soul without a home. I switch on the light and write these words. The dark goes away but she doesn't. I can even smell her, other people's smoke clinging to the *Trésor* — a sickly fog of peach, vanilla and ashes.

Every Gen X'er, sucking up *Poltergeist* to *Beetlejuice*, knows that ghosts are only done haunting when their unfinished business is completed and they're finally at rest.

There's no time for sleep.

Her unfinished business is her apology to you. And the apology means nothing without the whole story.

December 1994

It's Cait's second week of shifts and she isn't sure what she thinks about working in The Queen of Bohemia.

On the one hand – money.

On the other hand – seriously not cool.

The pub is this weird triangle with three different sets of punters to go with it: one bar for the theatre suppers, one for the postmen to have a swift afternoon half after their deliveries and, at the back of the building, the old queens muttering away, deciding if Cait's a *palone-omi*.

If she hadn't lost her job at the Pot. But, yeah, she had, hadn't she? The gaffer hadn't bought that her drink had been spiked, but the lie had been a shred of dignity to hide behind as she collected her last wage packet. Cait wouldn't be buying any more mystery confiscated little baggies from bouncers anymore, that's for sure. And whatever she had left was staying in her bedside cabinet. To say hospital food was unpalatable wasn't just a cliché. But that was last month, a lifetime ago. She rests her hand where the black fabric of her dress clings to her stomach. Then she pushes out her stomach muscles so her stomach is football size and the fabric around it goes shiny. Fucking hell. No wonder Rik got freaked out. With another missed period and the right story, that's some scary shit. She's almost convinced by it herself.

It's only seven but even so it's quiet for a Saturday night. Cait stares at the pale tan of the head barman's action slacks. Ronnie. He wipes down the bar and she knows for sure he'd be in danger of combusting at the smallest of stray sparks from an ashtray. She's got no idea why he even needs someone else in right now. Perhaps he just wants the company.

As he turns towards her Cait pulls in her stomach and shifts her gaze to her own legs, wrapped in black lacy tights, balances on one leg and rotates the other ankle, as if this is what she was doing all along. She looks up and Ronnie smiles to show his top row of perfect white teeth, falsies no doubt, and then tilts his head and hams up a frown, exaggerating the deep creases between his brows.

'Oi, Miss Caitlin. Stop practising your next gymnastics routine and wipe down the other bar. We all have other dreams you know but it shouldn't stop the work being done.'

The pan stick Ron uses to cover his acne scarring is thicker around his left eye tonight, but it still doesn't cover the swelling there.

Cait sighs, mirroring his theatrics.

'It's done already, Ronnie, there's no way I'm going to pick up another filthy dishrag just to ease your OCD.'

'Ay - don't be so slanderous about your very own Rhona's cleaning standards. Those dish cloths are all freshly laundered and you're just a moody cow.'

He starts walking into the theatre bar to see to a punter, telling her to *get a half, no more mind you, you lush, and get yourself a smile, because no punter wants to see a mood like that, even on a young and bloody gorgeous face.*

Cait pulls out a dimpled half pint pot and pours a little Guinness, her comfort drink. Her head is still pounding and her stomach is spitting acid, so that smile's going to be a tall order. She's got to go straight home tonight. No more fucking around with late night bars and taxis to God knows where. Maybe she wants Stadd. Maybe she doesn't. There isn't the heat there is with Rik, the urgent need to just have him. A little space will help. She knows Stadd's a nice guy, but his proximity to Rik is not good.

And there's the food situation. Another night of drinking will make the likelihood of being able to eat tomorrow slim. And Cait knows she's going to have to eat something soon, no matter how much her stomach burns and cramps, because when the double vision kicks in, functioning at work will become very hard indeed. She'll save money and maybe, just maybe, she could even start shaping herself a plan and get her poxy life back on track. Just because Aber and the Masters didn't work out doesn't mean her life's over.

So why does it feel like it right now?

Her Guinness hasn't even settled when Ronnie calls out to her, telling her that it's her boyfriend he's serving, dishy, but not his sort. Cait's guts immediately ramp up the burning. Rik? What the...?

"I take it you're just yanking my chain, Ron."

"Well, you're going to have to come around to the theatre bar and see for yourself."

As she turns, Cait makes out the figure unwrapping their scarf and lying it down on the bar. Stadd. Ronnie rests the first half of the Guinness he's been pouring next to the scarf, turns and smirks at Cait.

"Awww, how sweet," he says, "you two even drink the same drink."

Stadd's cheeks redden the same shade as Cait feels, as he insists he was just asking if Cait was around. Cait tells

Ronnie to stop stirring and his smirk widens to his full on *Steradent* grin as he orders Cait to pour the rest of Stadd's pint, not wanting to get in the way of the two love birds. As Ronnie walks past her to go back to the gay bar, he whispers so directly into her ear that she winces.

"I told those old queens there was no way a pretty girl like my new barmaid was a dyke."

Not knowing how to reply to such logic, Cait gets on with her job, picking up Stadd's glass and pouring the rest of his pint.

"So then, how did you know I was going to be here?"

His cheeks are still red and the same blotchiness has crept up his neck.

"Cait, it's hardly mysterious detective work. You told me last night. You did stay over."

Glancing around the bar to show she'd like to keep her private business private, she shushes him. Clearly there was nothing she could trust herself with when she'd been drinking. And now she'd set herself up to mope about here, somewhere painfully between hungover and sober, while Stadd sat on his drinking stool. The old queens would just lap that up. A bit of gossip. A bit of insight into the new girl's life.

"It won't be much fun for you sat there all night."

"Yeah, but I can have a drink and then we could go to Snobs afterwards."

"I don't know, Stadd. Might not be worth it by the time I've finished here."

Ronnie shouts from the next bar that she'll be done

by just turned eleven. And that they can take his brewery card too.

A light flicks on inside Cait at the thought of Snobs. Maybe at the thought of Rik. No, not Rik. Fucking hell, what is wrong with you woman? But if Stadd's here with her, Rik's probably not out at all. Haven't they always gone everywhere together? Mostly, she doesn't want to be stuck in this shithole a minute longer than she needs to be, and if this is the only way she can get out earlier, she'll do it.

"Okay, Stadd, you can thank Ronnie for twisting my arm. I'm going to let you take me out."

* * *

It's no surprise that the queue outside Snobs stretches around the corner. Same old. Cait hadn't been expecting to be out-out, so over the lacy cami top of her black dress she is at least wearing the thick black parka she bought for Aber.

Needlessly for Aber.

She's so quiet, Stadd asks if she's okay. She reminds him that she's been working, not drinking, and she needs a bit of time to warm up. It's the sort of lie that's entirely plausible because even Cait hasn't admitted what she's thinking. There's a fizz in her blood, and she can't hear herself think above its crackle.

The weak yellow light of the club's signage casts the queueing bodies into a different shade of darkness. Stadd shouts out at one of the shadows.

"Hey, fuckwit, are you letting us in the queue or what?"

Cait's eyes are drawn to a figure, shoulders rolled forward, shuffling from foot, and as her eyes adjust to the grey the figure is drawn out from the shadows. No coat. White t-shirt pulled over a tight chest. Dark curtained hair flopping over a tanned face.

Rik.

He shouts back.

"Stadd, man..." and stumbles a step towards them.

Cait can see his face clearly now, just as his sloppy brown eyes peek towards her and he says her name. She murmurs a reply, without forming any words in particular. She feels her hand firmly in Stadd's.

"Where's Diggy got to? Didn't bail on you, did he?" Stadd asks Rik.

"Parking up the car, mate."

"He's actually driving?"

"Antibiotics, apparently."

"Who's rotted his knob?"

"Heh. You know how country singers pay for their condoms? With Johnny Cash."

"Yeah, good one, Frank Skinner. No doubt Diggy's well pleased you're so pissed up."

"Stadd, man, I've hardly even started. Anyway, where have yous two been?"

"Cait's been at work."

Cait knows that Rik is looking at her, can feel that familiar sense of him taking her in that makes her queasy but, yes, excited.

"I didn't see you behind the bar."

There's a pause for Cait to fill, and when she doesn't, Stadd replies.

"She's working at the…"

Cait clasps back at Stadd's hand hard enough that it's clear it's not affection.

"I'm not at the Pot now, Rik. I'm working somewhere else."

And before Rik can crack any further into where Cait actually is working now, Stadd interrupts.

"Ahhh, there's Diggy. What's he waving at?"

"Tight cunt probably wants you to pay for his parking. I told him to piss off."

"I'll go tell him where to stick it."

As Stadd tries to loosen his fingers from Cait's, she holds onto them, says she'll come with him. But he doesn't want her to.

"I'll just be a sec."

As Stadd makes his way towards Diggy she's left with Rik. This one-to-one she's been trying to get from him all month, just delivered into her lap now, without trying.

Has she?

And what the hell would there be to want in this staggering mess, anyway? And yet there's that lurch of the stomach again. Please let it be disgust.

"It's you and Stadd now, is it?" Rik asks.

He's stopped staggering. In the year that she's known him he's moved from Kurt Cobain cardigans to some type of

Gallagher swagger. Hasn't every other fucker in the queue done the same, though? He pushes his hair out of his eyes and Cait sees that his fist is grazed and splattered with fresh red bruising.

Cait turns away from Rik. If she doesn't say anything, she can't say anything wrong. Instead her eyes follow Stadd approaching Diggy. Diggy with his vintage waffle cardigans and *Ben Sherman* shirts. His *Adidas* gazelles. Yet the poor bugger still looks a balloon with a blonde Brylcreemed slick-back. She very much doubts whether anybody had wanted to get close enough to rot his knob. Probably more like antibiotics for impetigo of the armpit.

She shrugs at Rik. He smirks and replies.

"I suppose I've seen you with worse than Stadd. What about that big spider hair guy?"

"Don't be such a fucking racist, Rik."

She sees that Stadd is holding out a handful of change in front of Diggy. Didn't he just say he wasn't going to give him any cash? So she's not the only one who acts one way in front of Rik, and closer to a decent human being when he's not up close. She hates that when Stadd is talking to Rik she can't even tell their voices apart.

Rik is waving his battered hand in her face now.

"So this was fun to go to work with today? Fending off the wise cracks from the knuckle-draggers."

"Where are you working now?"

"That construction site at the top of the Vale."

"And why do you think I'm interested in your hand?"

Diggy has turned back towards the car park, a huge

metal cage with the charm of an upturned trolley stuck in a canal. Stadd is making his way back to the queue. Rik won't stop talking.

"Are you fucking kidding me, Cait? If you're not with Stadd then you were doing a pretty good impression last night. Tonight, even."

Cait's still watching Stadd making his way to her. A girl at the back of the queue taps him on the shoulder as he walks by her. She's the sort of girl who doesn't know to grow out her long bob to stop looking like a mushroom, who doesn't even know to spray down the stray frizzy bits of hair. Stadd nods at the girl with a weak smile and walks another step. But the frizzy mushroom pulls at Stadd's coat sleeve and so he stops and turns towards her. Cait becomes vaguely aware that Rik's still talking at her and flicks her eyes back towards him.

"Cait, are you listening? I said my parents are going to chuck me out when they find out you're pregnant. It's only a matter of time, isn't it? Are you definitely pregnant?"

As her eyes grow more accustomed to the dim light, she sees how knackered Rik looks, dark circles ringing his eyes. His jaw is slack like it's too much effort to bring his pouty little lips together. Cait's hands fall to her stomach. She can't decide whether to suck it in or stick it out.

"It's about time all you man babies left home, anyway."

This vow not to reply to Rik isn't going well.

"Very mature. And does Stadd know you're up the duff?"

"I don't know, Rik. Maybe there's not been time to

talk about it yet."

Cait's too distracted to play with Rik anymore; even though he carries on talking at her somewhere at the edge of her awareness, his voice is low and grumbly and not hard to tune out. She's too distracted by the frizzy mushroom as she chats to Stadd, one arm resting on his, the other flailing around.

She knows that this ex, the wannabe, whatever she is, has seen Cait with Stadd and it's made her look at him differently. Now he'll be Stadd-who-can-get-with-Cait, with her cheekbones and rib cage ragged above her *Wonderbra* cleavage, her fat, smashed cherry lips, her long legs peeking through those lacy tights. Her coat wrapped around the secrets of her belly.

Cait knows exactly what her body looks like: she curates it every day in the long, smeary mirror on the back of the door to her bedsit. And she knows that the sharpness of her bones makes other women think she's in control of her life. Like fuck she is. She's in control of not eating, and her body does with that what it likes. The gushing periods. The no periods. The swelling stomach. The burning throat. The sharp stabbing pain of sex that only fades with alcohol. Fuckloads of alcohol.

"So, do I have to tell my folks you're pregnant or are you getting an abortion?" she hears Rik ask. And there it is. His favourite question.

"It's up to me, Rik. I don't have to tell you shit. You, on the other hand, can tell them whatever you like."

"You don't have to tell me shit when you want to bring my baby into the world? Are you even going to look at me?"

Not likely while the frizzy mushroom is trying to stare her out. The hand isn't just resting on Stadd's sleeve now, it's dragging the wool over his fingers.

"I don't want to bring your baby into the world, you wanker, I'm just not very stoked about having an abortion."

So she's going for it, the full-on allusion to a continuing pregnancy. Despite the negative test. She didn't know for sure she was going to keep the lie alive until she did it. Is it strictly a lie? There's been unprotected sex. There's been no period since. It's within the realms of possibility. And lying's such a great way of showing contempt. Man, what a rush. Like a whole day on just coffee. A little white baggie. Or silk knickers exiting the shop up her sleeve.

"Cait, for fuck's sake, listen to me. I can't afford a baby. We're too young. I mean, don't do this to me, man. Don't do it to yourself."

Rik grabs Cait's hand and she snaps her head round to look at him. He is cradling his other grazed fist against his chest. He is hanging his chin over the vee of his little t-shirt. He looks like his dog just got run over.

"I am not doing this to you or to me, Rik. We did this together."

There are warm hands on Cait's shoulders now. Thank fuck: Stadd's back. Cait turns to him, tilts her chin up for a kiss. He presses his mouth to hers, lips together, and then draws back.

"Sorry about that," he says. "Natalie. Kind of like my ex. She wouldn't take no for an answer. But she's going to have to."

Stadd kisses Cait again, hands on her cheeks then

slowly drawn down her body, over her bra, then out to her waist, her hips, resting on her arse. The heat that was rising in Cait cools, so her body is comfortable to be in again. She slips her hands inside his coat and around his waist, tucking her pelvis into his. She feels steady against his legs, against his mouth. He slips his tongue over hers first. The stout he's been drinking makes him taste like, what? Cait moves her tongue over Stadd's again to decide. Soil? Black crumbly soil you'd be curious to lick for a mad second. She knows Rik is watching. She doesn't doubt Natalie can't take her eyes off them too.

They kiss until Diggy's made his way back from the carpark and asks where Rik has got to. But he doesn't seem to be anywhere at all.

March 2018

This ghost won't accept my one-sided gaze. Nietzsche knew his stuff. When you gaze long into the abyss, the abyss gazes into you.

Stadd, when I tell her who I am, I tell you both.

My name is Caitlin. I am forty-four years old. I live in Birmingham. I have no children. I am not married. I am an ESOL teacher.

Today the weather was sunny but cold.

Today I am feeling...

This is where I stumble. I think about the flashcards I give to my learners. The miming game I get them to play. *Show me what happy looks like. What about bored? Angry? Sad?*

Now match the feelings to these sentences.

It is sunny she is on the beach.

Tell me, how does she feel?

She has no friends. She has nothing to do.

How does she feel?

She is running a long way.

How does she feel? How does she feel?

How does she feel?

Stadd, I'm sorry I didn't know how I felt.

Today, I was the woman who walked along Ceredigion Bay, framed by velvet green mountains and that ocean plush with dolphins, porpoises, seals. The same sea, the same coast I ran from when I was twenty-one. But I came back. Came back every year for my solo writing retreat. Call it my sick sense of humour.

It is the same bay, but I am not the same woman. This woman is not a ghost. She has landed in her body at last.

It's 2am and the ghost has finally passed out. I switch off the light.

Can you see me now?

3.

March 2018

My alarm went off at 5 this morning while everything was still dark– lack of sleep wouldn't stop me from getting up. Routine's what keeps me together now. If I'm tired after lunch I will nap. Every morning – breakfast (yes, I eat breakfast now), journalling, sun salutations, and, if it's not a teaching day, back to the page with that big-barrelled pen.

Does knowing that I try to make myself better and shinier, qualify as part of this apology? I didn't use you as a prototype to treat a slew of other men in a shitty way. I've just stuck to disappointing, and being disappointed by, my lovers in a myriad of vanilla ways. But those little ways still manage to stab. Over time, I've learnt to keep the drama on the page.

When I applied for my Masters in Aberystwyth, I had so wanted the freshness of a new start by the sea, to play out my fantasy of being a real writer. And real writers drank too much, fell in love too easily and were heading for their own special tragedy.

Clichés? I was full of them.

But the unwholesomeness, the dirtiness was in me, not in the city I was escaping, and I took it to Aber with me. Aber was not fresh because Cait was not fresh. What kind of Brummie drama did you take to Oz and Sooz, Stadd? Or was it all out of your system by then?

I was so afraid of looking like I didn't know what I was doing. I couldn't even admit I was baffled by Aber's weird library system. It took me a fortnight to find my pigeon-hole and my only post, a letter from my mom. Did I know that Dolores from the Cranberries had bleached her hair now? And when was I going to send her a cheque for my half of the last electricity bill? Because there's no way I'd already given her the cash. She wouldn't forget that, and if I ever wanted to come home again...

With this fear and this smallness, and just one month into my course I had an epiphany – I didn't need to be in academia to be a writer. I could move back to Brum, where the booze and the men flowed freely, the stuff of a real, writerly life. And I didn't need to live with my mom. But I did need to write to be a writer, and not stuff the holes with aimless journalling, with drinking and with men. With Rik. And with you.

This B&B room today, with its smell of bleach and salty dampness, and the single-glazed, whitewashed window that looks out to a distant roiling sea, is the doppelganger of the room I had during my post-grad Aber minute. It's bare except for the bed I sit on, and a wardrobe that I don't need to use.

Yesterday's jeans and soft charcoal sweater are folded on top of my suitcase, lying behind the door. The sun's rising now in a mauve sky, screaming with starlings. And we're not the only early risers. I'm four floors up and outside the window I see a bright green diamond kite whipping around. Not very skilfully. Perhaps a parent with their small child? I can't see the beach from here; still the sea rustles in my ears. When I write about us, Stadd, it doesn't feel like I'm writing about the past. It's like I'm predicting the future, the grimmest future I can think of, from my first Aber room.

January 1995

It's funny how underwear becomes provocative in someone else's presence. As she switches on the light in her bedsit, the first thing Cait sees is the violet bra caught around the cupboard handle, an aesthetic nod to the size of her tits and her desire to push them up and together. She grabs at the bra's straps with one hand and opens the cupboard by the edge of the split plywood door with the other, chucking the bra inside. A pair of nearly matching knickers falls at her feet. This morning, the staining on the gusset was just another yeast infection, but now it becomes an obscene admission of her own juices. She scoops them up and disappears them with the tangle of clean and dirty, mostly dirty, clothes.

Stadd is a couple of steps behind her, shutting the door. Cait doesn't know what he's seen, discrete to her fuck ups as he is. In a month of drinking and chatting every type of bollocks together, this is the first time Stadd has been inside – her home? Cait struggles to call it that. Her room. The place where she keeps her stuff. The place where she sleeps since she decided not to admit defeat to her mother on dropping out of her Masters at Aber.

Living with her mother had been bad enough during her undergrad years. Aber was supposed to be the moment of growing up, the spreading of wings and using the middle feathers to give Mother the finger. *Except I couldn't hack it could I*, thinks Cait, *couldn't get myself organised, couldn't take the loneliness, not a single man interested, not even any intrigue*. A craving for a man like a sickness, even bigger than her desire to write and create.

She hates her neediness, so she has built a wall

around it, a wall of looking like she doesn't give a fuck. And now Stadd's come back to this dive with her, this dingy little hole off the Washwood Heath Rd, and Cait has to see her life through his eyes. Like she doesn't give a fuck about the chintzy autumn leaves peeling from the walls. Like the swirling carpet that doesn't easily distinguish between pattern and staining doesn't make her queasy. That her sad little single bed with papers, cassettes, orange-spined paperbacks and make-up strewn across its lumpy duvet just shows how she chooses to live and is not a substitute for a life she's not up to.

Cait hasn't even got her own bog here, let alone anywhere to bathe, which means her showering habits have become as irregular as her meals. She didn't choose it. She feels like she's forgotten how to eat. When she lived with her mom she ate what she was given. But all she's got now is a sink with limescale on the taps, and a kettle. She's had to make a life where whore's baths and a hot drink make do for the lack of home comforts.

"I've got no booze," she says to Stadd, collecting the dirty mugs from around her bed. "Do you want a cup of tea?"

He nods and starts to gather some of the shit from Cait's bed. She hasn't changed the dark purple sheets since she moved here three months ago. And seventy days now without a period.

"A bit presumptuous, aren't you?"

Stadd stops gathering, his hand across an old NME cover, a finger lying across PJ Harvey's cleavage. Cait feels the protective wall around her, crumbling.

"Why, is there somewhere else to sit?" he asks.

"What a surprise. You're not just here for a cup of tea after all."

"Doesn't look like I'm getting one either way, does it?"

Cait shrugs her shoulders and holds the mugs over the sink. Stadd drops the paper back on her bed and moves behind her, placing his hands on her waist. She closes her eyes.

"You don't have to explain to me why you don't want me on the bed, Cait. There's a lot of stuff going on. Big decisions to make."

She's picturing Natalie and her frizzy hair, what her bedroom might be like, wondering if she'd been allowed to have Stadd on her bed, in it even. She's seeing floral bedding, ruffled blinds, a huge pastel blue teddy bear that's meant to look ironic. Stadd's hand dutifully rubbing at her cotton pants after a respectful period of kissing. Her mom's gel ball air freshener wafting under the door. Her imagination is doing its best to block out Rik. Cold concrete rubbing against Cait's arse. People waiting for the bus on the other side of the municipal flower planter. Rik's hand over her mouth. Could a life really start like that?

"There's nothing to decide. If a baby wants to come, it'll come."

That cool, clean reckless feeling. Like being fucked in public. Like pretending there was nothing that could make her life any worse.

"It's not all out of your hands, Cait. A baby will complicate the fuck out of your life. Having a baby here?"

"Because you don't want me to have a baby?"

35

"That's only your business, like your bad, bad taste in music. You listen to PJ Harvey screeching for fun, do you?"

"A bit too angry for the pope of mope?"

"Are you an angry grrrrl?" he asks, and starts to kiss the back of her neck. Cait tips the dregs of the mugs into the sink, places them down softly there.

Stadd moves away and takes his coat off. Laying it on the bed he holds out his hands, palm side up. The red lining of his coat glistens like a split knuckle. Cait's cringing as she reads his softened face, parted lips showing the little gaps between his teeth, but she takes his hand so he can pull her towards the bed. Do what's asked. Saying no now gets messy.

He kneels in front of Cait and she has to stoop her neck to get to his mouth. Kissing, yes, she can lose herself in kissing. For weeks she's been trying to remember what Stadd's aftershave reminds her of, and as his face reaches up to hers, the memory is there. The rain lashing down through those massive cedar trees. That smell flooding the school tent, like pine needles smashed into oranges.

Smoothing down Cait's hair, Stadd touches her cheek. The lightbulb is shitty enough for Cait to allow herself to be looked at close up, without panic. His other hand pushes into the small of her back, shuffling her closer. There's that feeling again, like the world's slowing down, that it might not be too late. Without looking or feeling, she knows he is hard now. And for the journey he's made, out of his way, kissing's not going to be enough, is it?

She drops to her knees in front of Stadd, starts to kiss his neck, slides herself down his chest, slides her fingers between the buttons in his fly. He presses his hands over hers to stop the unbuttoning, lifts her chin upwards, tells her to lie on the bed. She can't find the words to make it stop. Never knew them to start with.

She lies on the lining of his coat, slippery against her silky grey dress. He is rolling off her tights. He has laid his glasses down on her bedside cabinet and now he is kissing her thighs. Cait's chest is thumping because she knows what he's trying to do, pushes at his head. Oh this is worse. Does he think she's teasing? He bites, softly, in reply.

Her knickers have been pushed to the side and his tongue is on her now, she thinks, but she doesn't know for sure, because she's not in her body now. She's all up in her head. She's in a little corner of the ceiling, the one with the least cobwebs, looking down.

She stays very still. She doesn't play up, not that Cait objects to a moan and a clench to get out of a tight situation, but right now she is too mortified to play act. From her little corner of the ceiling she sees a dreamy look on Stadd's face and she is embarrassed by his devotion. She's not washed since this morning.

It happens despite herself, a warmth, an itchiness in the pit of her stomach. She sees it rise as a pink patch spreads across her rib cage. It keeps rising until it prickles at her neck and cheeks. And, for just a moment, her whole body makes a fist then loosens to an open palm.

She doesn't want to look at Stadd. She lets him roll up her tights, put his glasses back on. She lets him draw her up to a sitting position and kiss her on the mouth. Ugh the taste, like a cheap, sour mash. But she keeps on kissing just to stop him looking her in the eye.

Later, Stadd calls a taxi on the payphone in the hall and when he comes back they lie together on the bed, Cait tucked under his arm, dozing, until headlights flash three times through the drawn curtains and they both start at the sound of a horn.

**

In the sloppy, wet blackness there's a banging, a relentless banging, that makes the dark sea of sleep recede, leaving Cait washed up and awake, mouth like sand and her insides stinging like a bellyful of salt-water. The door. Some bastard's banging on the bastard door.

"Oi – OI! You in number 3 – it's the phone for you. I'm not a fucking secretary, you lazy bint."

Cait shouts, tries to shout, in reply. Some strangled sound comes out of her mouth that at least makes the banging stop.

She stumbles to the door, still in last night's slip dress, and then checks herself in the mirror that hangs there. Licking the outside of her index fingers with what spit she can muster, she runs them first under her eyes and then her dry tongue over her lips. But what about the mop? Every feathery layer is competing for attention, pointing in its own direction. It's too big a job. Her hair will have to stay as it is.

In the hallway, the payphone's handset dangles towards the worn floral carpet on its twisted wire. Cait picks it up and rubs the mouthpiece along the hem of her dress. It leaves a brownish smear. It doesn't stop the receiver smelling of a tangle of bad breath. Cait breathes through her mouth to avoid gagging.

"Hey – it's Cait," she hears her voice croak out.

"Well, thank crikey for that – I thought it was another one of my heavy breather calls."

It's takes a moment for her brain to register but there's only one person alive who still uses crikey. Ronnie. Fuck, had she missed her shift already?

"I'm so sorry Ron, just give me fifteen minutes to get sorted and I'll be on the next bus."

The exertion of cranking herself out of bed meets the panic of missing a shift. There's a puddle gathering in her cleavage and a rancid cumin smell being mobilised at her armpits.

"Will you now, young Miss Caitlin? It's a bit presumptuous cos I don't even want you here yet."

"What? What is it then, Ron? What's with the dawn chorus call?"

She's just confused now, and as her belly cramps up, the heat and dampness are rushing out of her. Neck, pits, crotch, crack. Disgusting. Just disgusting

"It's ten thirty, Cait – I think the birds are already having their first nap. The story, my lovely, is that his nibs has got a cob on. When I was doing the bar rota for this week it seems I forgot about his Dad's 70th birthday do tonight and I rostered myself on."

Cait knows he is talking about his partner, the moustachioed one. But what is his name? No, there's only his Magnum PI moustache floating behind her eyes.

"So you want me to work tonight, Ronnie?"

"I'd be ever so grateful if you did. I'll cover you this lunchtime. He's having a right hissy fit. Those butches are the worst at throwing their toys out of the pram. And don't let anyone tell you any differently."

Cait rubs at her dampening forehead. She knows that a hissy fit would be the politest way of describing the outburst that the moustached one has probably had. She hopes poor Ron is stocked up on ice and his orange panstick.

"Not a problem, Ron – when do you want me on?"

Ronnie carries on speaking but Cait is distracted, having turned to see one of her neighbours has let himself in through the door behind her. He has a heavy, vinegary odour which fills the hallway.

She pulls her free arm across herself, raising her shoulders and hollowing out her chest to make herself smaller as he walks past her. The neighbour is swinging a white carrier bag of *Tennents Super*, Cait presumes from the can already opened in his hand. He takes a long swig and grins at her.

"That's a nasty stain you've got on your pretty clothes there, number three."

Cait pinches the receiver between her neck and shoulder and rubs at the smear that the phone has left on her dress.

The neighbour sucks his thin bottom lip against stripy teeth.

"Number three you are funny," he says dragging out the first syllable of funny. "That's not half your troubles. Looks like Aunt Flo's back in town and she's angry as fuck."

He chuckles to himself, as if it's the funniest thing he's heard in a while and takes another swig from his big blue can, climbs the stairs.

Cait's reaches round to the back of her dress and when she brings her hand round again, tears up at the red-brown ooze smeared across her palm.

March 2018

I think we've both noticed by now that this is not a memory. Too many holes already. Later, there'll be too many tidy bows. It's a story. I'm not just a rambling journaller anymore, I've learnt how to shape a narrative. Though it's bloody hard to shape it around a character who doesn't know what she wants. And how do you like this story so far? I doubt you're sitting comfortably. I'm sure not. My poor hand is cramping again, this time with a cringe reflex.

My apology is a curation of thoughts, the embellishment of memories. I'm gathering it all around a theme and the theme is: Caitlin, what a piece of shit. Aber's always been the place I come to that conclusion. Because even though I've worked hard to be better, there's a satisfaction in punishing myself for having been a monster. I am the torturer and the tortured. The top and the bottom.

Have you heard of confirmation bias, Stadd? It's the theory that we all tend to search for information to back up what we already believe. It affects what we remember too and how we interpret our memories.

Your parents seemed to like you. There was a warmth between you, even though I could see they were restrained, not wanting to embarrass you in front of this new girl. How your dad asked, with a flush, if I knew that you all worked at the same factory plant. The way your mom lent in at the table her hand rising like a twitch, before she rested back in her chair to tell you, instead, about the toast crumb on your cheek. The way they didn't demand cash from you in front of your mates.

The belief I'd always gathered my thoughts around

was that I was a burden to be around, and to have to love me was a terrific task nobody should have to undertake for free. I could be tolerated at best. And if anybody saw the me who lurked underneath, they wouldn't like her. Well, here she is, in the story of that hidden me, the ghost in the machine. I think it's clear I went out of my way to be un-loveable.

Tenderness. A kind look. It's what you gave me, Stadd, and I didn't have prior experience to interpret it. Confirmation bias. I wasn't looking for it, so I didn't see it. But as I write from this room and its uncertain place in time and space, it's what my mind's eye sees now.

Outside the window the sky is clear. I watch the kite hovering within the frame like a huge green leaf against the blue before it whips up, the tendril of its line unspooling, and disappears. I'm not going to be fooled by the sun. I'll wrap up before I go out, tuck in my scarf, because today will be like yesterday and its ferocious bite. I'm going out to find a café, to write some more of this apology, to have some lunch and fasten my stomach to this plane, make sure my mind doesn't get untethered from the writing hand.

4.

January 1995

You have to be grateful for any quiet bar shift. And with the bleeding and the lack of Ronnie, Cait's very grateful, even more grateful that she's on her way home now. As she makes careful steps through another cold night in town, fast enough that she won't miss her last bus, but slow enough not to encourage a gush of blood into the last *Always Ultra* she's got on her, Cait wonders if Ronnie had a good time at the family party.

What it's like for him to be around his boyfriend's folks? Do they know Ronnie and Mr Moustachio are a couple, or is it politely assumed they are just good friends? For that to be plausible, Ronnie would have to turn himself down by fifty percent. Seventy five percent to be on the safe side.

And wasn't that where Stadd was tonight too? Well, not with Ronnie, but a meal for his Nan and Grandad's wedding anniversary. January was a fucking weird time for so many celebrations. Nobody chooses when to be born, but choosing January as a wedding date? Bleak.

Also bleak: this clotty, gushy forty-two days late bleeding. Cait knows this is going to be a fucker of a period to have with the communal bedsit bog. As she passes the darkened windows of *Miss Selfridge*, and that silver crocheted belly top she's going to have to pilfer if she wants it, she starts to calculate what will be the optimum ratio of clothes to wear to bed tonight. She doesn't want to wake up sweating and claustrophobic, but she also needs any emergency missions to the bathroom to have her covered and decent. And please, please, please don't let the bog get jammed up again.

She remembers a spotty pair of pyjamas and a towelling gown she used to have when she lived with her mom. Was that the year that she'd wanted a guitar that she'd never got? Cait had been so narked by that Christmas present. Now nothing she has seems practical or warm, except this black parka coat, but even that's starting to rip inside the pockets where she's been digging for warmth.

Cait glances at the King's Head clock on High St to check she's making good enough time to get her bus, but her eyes are drawn to a coatless figure stumbling across the new pedestrianised street. She knows it's Rik, even though he looks smaller than she remembers. Maybe it's because he's usually backed up by two, three, four mates, or maybe he's being swallowed by the space. But is there actually less of him though? Is he losing weight?

It's not surprising to cross someone familiar at this time of night. If there's a circle of midnight bus regulars, then her and Rik are the inner ring. But that bastard in particular always turns up at times like these. Right from the first time she'd met him, her heart all bust up, and he'd pinched her arse as she was collecting a tower of pint glasses in the Pot. Oh, that started it all didn't it? The first domino. And then when she'd crawled back from Aber, he was ready to take her back to his gaff because his folks were away that weekend. Of course she'd see Rik tonight, on this first night of blood leaking out of her, Stadd-less, when she knew the baby charade had to stop.

He is stumbling towards her: vulnerable. It's not a new look on Rik, but usually Cait senses it's calculated, a mask to slip on when there are knickers to be gotten in to. That tilt of his head and his sloppy puppy eyes, like his apology for pinching her arse and then somehow, she'd ended up with him later. Despite her first threat of smashing the pint glasses over his head if he ever tried anything like that again.

But this look is different.

This isn't Rik's mask of vulnerability. Is it actual vulnerability?

"Cait, Cait," he cries out, hands reaching out for hers, but she keeps them tucked in the ripped lining of her pockets. "Tell me what the fuck is happening. I need to know, man. I'm dying here."

The sentence Cait has to speak is ripening in her mouth, and she knows it will be the greatest gift Rik has received in his life. She delivers it without wrapping paper, without bows.

"I'm not pregnant, Rik."

"Oh, thank fuck, Cait, thank fuck."

Maybe his questions will come later but for now there's none. He doesn't ask if she was ever pregnant, if there was an abortion, a miscarriage, or if it was all a mistake. All he needs is the simple answer she's already given. He lunges towards her and before she can brace herself his arms are across her arse and he's swinging her round.

Cait wishes everything inside her wasn't singing out as Rik's arms press into her, as her stomach is pushed up against his chest, but it is, it is, even with her knowing there's the risk that he could come away bloodstained. At least the point about not being pregnant would be made.

Rik puts Cait down in front of him and holds her hands, which are out of her pockets now to steady the spinning street. She is relieved to see the clean, tanned skin of his forearms, his stainless white t-shirt.

"My dad was going chuck me out," he says, and although when he's said this before Cait has thought it was an exaggeration, she believes him now, sees that yes, there is less of him, he has lost weight and that can't be for no reason. "And I haven't been picking up much work, so I didn't know what the fuck I was going to do."

Cait agrees, yes, it is good news, but as she replies she can see that Rik's openness is already starting to close down. He lets go of her hands.

"Well this is good news for Stadd," he adds.

"I've been at work," Cait replies, "So I've not seen him yet. You?"

And as she asks, Cait remembers his family do and regrets looking like she doesn't know what Stadd's up to.

The King's Head clock says there's time, just, for a hug before Cait has to get to her bus. Rik's head leans on her shoulder. For one beat, the dark hair clipped into his nape and the smell of burnt matches makes her heart thump faster, and then a new feeling. Softness? The way he's at rest against her is gentle. Fuck. Is this a tender emotion that they're sharing together? With her arms around Rik she feels no tension in the thick muscles across his back. This is a different man from all the other times he's been this close to her, when that heat between them has been so fierce she's wanted to exit her own skin.

As Cait walks away from Rik, she wonders who she'll ever be able to talk to about this, the fire between her and Rik that never leads anywhere. It is not even satisfied by sex. It especially isn't satisfied by sex. It is a craving for him to look at her, to touch her, to be next to her, that is as much post-coital as pre-coital. It is a longing that starts over even as he squirms his dick back out of her, every drunken time they've fucked. It's like the burning in her stomach that just gets worse when she eats. The hungrier she is, the more it hurts to try and fill her belly.

The bus draws up to the stop with a belch of diesel just ahead of Cait. A rocker couple in the queue, with the same black leathers and the same icy shade of long blonde hair hold hands as they stroll forward. They stop to kiss as they realise the poor bugger ahead of them, with her dirty, too small anorak and her bird's nest hair, is scrabbling with her bus fare, counting out the coppers, holding up the queue. Cait can see the heat in the kiss, but then as they take their seats they laugh like they're best mates.

Stadd has so quickly become her best friend. She looks forward to seeing him, wants to hang out with him, be with him, let him see to her hangovers. Cait can tell Stadd everything. But now he's complicated it all by sticking his head between her legs. She has never felt more distant from him.

Cait's stomach is throbbing as it squeezes to gets rid of seventy days' worth of deception and indecision. At least she can't feel the burning of her stomach acid over the pain of her womb being wrung out. The bus seat is hard underneath her pelvis. She just wants to get home and then, with a jolt, she remembers where she lives now and squeezes her eyes together to prevent another type of leaking she'd like to prevent happening in public.

March 2018

It's so much easier to write when there are people to watch going about their everyday stuff.

I've nursed this latte for a few hours now, but I can't decide what I want to eat. Something like the old burning starts to rumble in my stomach.

When I was fifteen my mother told me to make sure I didn't have sex before I got married. That's how old we are — parents still told their kids that. It was too late for me by then. And that philosophy hadn't kept my parents together, but now I know that wasn't what it was about.

It's easy to stay chaste when you don't feel desire. Had my mom ever let herself feel desire for a man? I couldn't imagine it. Not just my mother, but my aunts, too. Men were there for women to gripe about, as if my mother never had a choice about who chose her.

Did I choose Rik, though? Did I choose you, Stadd? Can I remember who it was that I actually wanted, or do I just want a nice, neat story for this apology?

There's nothing I want to eat at this café. Besides, I need to take a long walk before I'm ready to write the next part. It was naïve to think I could conjure you back, without Rik at your heels.

5.

Definition of *apology*

1a: an admission of error or discourtesy accompanied by an expression of regret:

a written *apology*.

b: apologies *plural*: an expression of regret for not being able to do something:

I'm not able to do the right thing. Sending you my *apologies*.

2a: something that is said or written to defend something that other people criticise:

DEFENSE. The story is an *apology* for infidelity.

b: EXCUSE SENSE 2a.

3 *informal*: a poor substitute or example:

MAKESHIFT. I was a poor *apology* for a lover.

February 1995

It's one a.m. and Rik and Cait are leaving
Snobs together. As they climb the stairs, the rows of
white mannequin faces that decorate the walls gaze, the
expressionless masks staring as the cashier prints Rik's hand,
and then Cait's, with the S of the red club stamp. As Rik
pushes open the exit to another cold, black night he reaches
back with his other arm, and Cait slips her fingers into his,
entwining their branded hands together.

They could have spoken inside the club. There
were quieter spots in the club where they could have gone:
the corridor that linked the two club rooms, with its stools
and mirrors and neon lighting, the large black square of
the stairwell, propped against the fag machine. So when
Cait agrees with Rik to go outside, they both know it isn't
necessary if all that's on their minds is talking.

There is a pattern. A ritual. A ceremony. Tonight,
they do not diverge from it. Rik leads them to a place he
thinks is remote enough. Rik and Cait do not speak while they
walk there, walking away from the club, away from the gauzy
streetlights, walking away from the other drunks and their
screwy plans. The quiet is important. It helps Cait to keep her
mind empty.

Cait should not desire Rik, but she does.

Rik doesn't want to be with Cait.

He just wants to be in her.

She knows. The silence fences off these thoughts.

It's ten past one in the morning and Cait is lying on
her back on the second floor of the big metal car park. She is

the sandwich filling between Rik and the concrete floor. Her legs are splayed open at the knees. Her tights are rolled down to the tops of her boots, keeping her ankles shackled in place. Cait is the one who shackled them there.

This is what she wants. Her lips and jaw are numb with kissing, her mouth and Rik's smashed together over and over. The back of her head bears too hard into the bitter, gritty floor. The icy air is thin and burns her nostrils, but Rik is on top of her, his stomach hot against her, shoving into her. Quick, quick, it's freezing. Shit, is someone coming back to their car?

Scratch into his back, gasp into his ear. Squeeze his hips between her thighs. This is what she wants.

He groans and shudders.

This is what she wants.

* * *

As Cait steps back in Snobs, the change in temperature has got her sweating –that cumin stink is gathering at her armpits again. Her thighs feel slippery and scratchy all at once, her twisted tights rub as she walks towards Stadd and Diggy.

Stadd passes her another vodka-lime and his fingers jump and curl back towards him but he doesn't mention how cold her hand is. She raises the glass to her lips and swigs away the taste of Rik's Marlboro.

She's trying to ground herself, but the club is a mess of images, the red swirling lights making their way through the darkness, the puffs of dry ice, the dust motes hanging in the air, anonymous bodies everywhere, some still, others thrashing in time to the guitars. Stadd, and his quiff, his

Crombie coat, are always easy to spot, but she can't see Diggy
now. The drink starts to cool her down and then she makes
out Rik, resting his Newky Brown against the sticky surface
of a podium. He's staring at the bottle like he's trying to get
into it, or maybe wondering what's going to come out. Is that
Natalie pulling at his arm? Cait's stomach squeezes.

Rik is next to them now, stretching up to Stadd's
ear. The red light is swirling over Cait and both men rush
into darkness, until her eyes adjust again. First the light starts
as a splodge on Rik's torso, the bottle he holds now pressed
against his crotch, and then spreads out to Stadd's nodding
head, smiling, pushing his glasses up, as if he agrees with this
whole fucking mess.

Stadd is holding Cait's hands, rubbing them in his.
She wants to say sorry, but then she'll have to say what she's
sorry for. It's just easier if she shuts her eyes. She knows her
hands are still freezing. Stadd uses them to pull her closer to
him, wrapping his arms around her.

Cait doesn't move.

Stadd pushes up her fringe with his nose and kisses
her damp forehead. She knows she'll taste of salt and smoke.
She knows she'll taste of Rik.

She opens her eyes and Rik is sucking at his cigarette
as he strikes a match. Behind them, Diggy passes Natalie a
bottle. Rik is looking at Cait and widens those sloppy eyes as
he catches a light.

* * *

Is this finally rock bottom now? Lower than the
concrete floor of a car park. After ten days on her lumpy
mattress, in that old familiar sticky tar pit of self-loathing,

down to only black coffee to fill her stomach, Cait had at last taken one of Ronnie's calls. Not out of guilt or decency, but just to get him to stop calling because it's pissing off her neighbours. Maybe number 5 does know somebody skilled in the art of the personalised petrol bomb. Better not risk it.

That phone call has led to this, riding a Wednesday evening bus and shuffling across town to The Queen, in her longest, baggiest dress. She's here to collect her last wage packet and, as Ronnie put it, have a heart to heart that's long overdue. Her stomach's past the worst burning, but it's hard to trust what she's seeing right now. It can't really be three of her hands resting on the smeared brass plate as she tries to gather what's left of her. She tucks in the end of a strip of old cami top that's wrapped around her hair, then stares at the ragged varnish stains left in the middle of her twelve, nine, fifteen fingernails.

Breathe. Fill those lungs with the city grime. The face is a mask that will save. Thick wings of liquid eyeliner and those smashed cherry lips will work hard not to reveal any truth. And there's Plan B too. That baggie of the white stuff that's been living inside her bedside cabinet, now nuzzled between her left tit and her bra. She'll definitely never do that again. But just in case.

Ronnie asks the moustachioed one to watch the bar and beckons Cait into his office, a walk-in cupboard where the phone, the safe and Ronnie's ledgers live. He's not his normal fizzy self, perhaps this is how it goes before he gives a bollocking. Should have seen that coming.

As she pulls shut the concertinaed door, she hears the safe's dial whizzing round. The little brown envelope of her wages is already in Ronnie's hand. He turns to her, smoothing down the cropped fringe of his sandy toupé, and takes a deep breath, exhales. Stale fags, coffee breath and dehydration rush into the tiny space. *Breathe deeply, Cait. But not too deeply. Keep the eyes focused on Ronnie's powder blue tie. Hold on, is it too wide to focus on?*

"So are you going to tell me where you've been, young Miss Caitlin?"

Cait shrugs. What's she going to say – I've been trapped in the sticky pit of my own despair?

"Have you been holed up with your be-quiffed one? It's been most strange not having him around. I've not had to change the Guinness barrel once this week."

"No, it's not like that."

Cait's regretting the choice to focus on Ronnie's tie now. It's too similar in colour to his shirt. She needs to find something with a clearer outline. That new chip in his dentures.

"Is this your idea of a heart to heart?"

"You're the one who wanted the heart to heart, Ron. I just need my wages."

"Well, man cannot live on bread alone, nor woman, and it doesn't even look like you're getting any bread. That old hippy dress isn't fooling me, you bag of bones. Why isn't that fella of yours helping you take better care of yourself?"

"I don't have a boyfriend."

"Oh man-friend, lover, life partner, whatever you kids say nowadays."

"Ronnie. There's no man now."

"Oh my poor lovely. It's all starting to make sense

now." Ronnie hugs Cait but the angle is too awkward for her to hug him back. "You know I've told his nibs he's on his last chance too. I'm not putting up with his tantrums any more, family problems or not."

Ronnie tells her that when he was young and lovely, he wishes he'd known he could have had anybody that he wanted instead of getting himself well and truly in the groove of pining after wrong 'uns. He tells her that he's missed her and he wants her to come back to work.

Cait thinks perhaps she can do this. Perhaps she just needs someone, somewhere to not think that she's a sack of shit. Perhaps it will be the lift she needs.

He insists she works the Friday shift. Ronnie isn't going to let Cait slip away that easily. She's back in the fold.

6.

March 2018

All afternoon the clouds have been gathering. I
walked the loop around Aber from Penglais to the grounds
of the Castle ruin. The rain couldn't be measured in drops:
everything was just wrapped in a damp sheet. Finally, I settled
down to write in another coffee chain. Another latte with its
heart logo foam in its bucket-sized mug and I could have been
anywhere in the world. But where I was, was on my back
between the concrete and Rik that first time that I put ten
thousand miles between me and you. Oh the shit I've written
today.

I don't need to apologise to Rik. And if I needed to
it wouldn't be hard. There'd be no spell needed. The few
nights a year I go into Birmingham, up he pops. We raise
eyebrows, nod. Neither of us wants to step back into that
boiling pot again. Too old for that crap. And what would I
need to apologise to him for anyway? We were playing the
same game.

But Ronnie. I'd love to have said sorry to Ronnie. I
doubt he's longer with us. He's certainly not at The Queen
anymore - that place lost its old flavour a long time ago. It
still sells itself as a theatre pub, but it's all beards and craft
beer; cocktail master classes. Those old *omi-palones* have long
cleared out. So legend has it, The Queen of Bohemia has its
own ghost. Yeah, mate. That'll be me. The dybbuk of Cait.

I want to tell you how I fucked Ronnie over too.
How after he tried to gather me up, showed me decency
when I'd not showed him any, I did go back and do that shift.
I also saved that white baggie for the occasion: if only speed

obliterated memory like a bottle of vodka. Ronnie didn't call me again after that one. I see now I was pushing him to see how far he'd go in accepting me. Being off my face on a working shift? I found my line. Again.

But come on now. Come with me, Stadd. Let's round this thing off, back to the last time I remember seeing you. It's about time our unfinished business is finally done. Let's put all the ghosts to rest.

Cait doesn't know the girl serving the Guinness, with her top knot and her under shave, her pouty blue lips. All change here at the Pot. The staff always turns over quickly, Cait is just another old face now. An old face that's braving it for the first time since the sacking. Thank fuck the gaffer isn't around. But still Cait's hands fidget on the bar as she waits to pay. She's here to bump into Stadd. To look like it's casual.

She finds a place to stand in a dark corner, under where the DJ's booth hangs like a pulpit. It's a bit loud, but her brain needs the scrambling. And it's a place she can emerge from to be spotted, rather than look like the one who's doing the spotting. Of course, if Stadd's here then Rik won't be far away. She takes a gulp of Guinness, rubs at her purple painted nails with her thumb. It'll be fine. Rik's out of her system now. She can't live in the pit forever.

There's only a scattering of people to scan. But, yes. Stadd's here, his back to where she stands. That coat. That hair, taller than anyone he's standing with. Rik. Diggy. She recognises some other guys but can't put a name to them. She looks at her pint and sees three fingers full have gone already. Funds are low so there's an equation to balance. Drunk enough to have the balls to walk up to Stadd, but avoid spending her limited cash up front.

And then there's the other weight on the scales: she can't be too drunk and slip up in what she's going to say. But it'll be okay. It's fine. Why can't she stop swaying then? Just make sure it's in sync with the beat, avoid looking too much of a weirdo. It's not like Rik would tell Stadd about what happened, so why worry? But it niggles that Stadd hasn't been looking for her, hasn't called her, and Ronnie said he hadn't even been to The Queen to see her. Fuck no, don't think of Ronnie now. There's only so much shame to shoulder at a time, no need to think about how she fucked up there.

So why else would Stadd have kept away if he didn't know about her and Rik? Except he can't. But, shit, could he? Rik would be too chicken to tell him. The swaying's not enough now, she's stepping from foot to foot.

Perhaps she'll need a whole pint to talk to him. To oil her flirting valve. At least she's eaten today. She can't go over with an empty glass though. Too weird.

Cait touches her flat belly exposed between jeans and her new silver crocheted top, turns her belly button ring so the ball sits flat. Stadd's silhouette is so distinctive, sloping shoulders always in that Crombie coat, his tall hair. Her eyes trace the square of his neckline before she clocks the fact that Rik isn't with the crowd. She's got a third of a pint left in her glass. What she's had will have to be enough now. She walks into the light and over to Stadd.

From the look on his face as she approaches, he hadn't seen her yet. Not everyone scans a room like Cait. Not many people do. His smile is smaller, shyer than she's used to seeing, that flush she remembers, though, rises on his neck. There's a lurch in her chest like it's the first time she's felt how much she fancies him. So distracting that how she greets him is pathetic.

"Well, hello stranger."

"Same to you. Cait, isn't it?"

Cait wrinkles up her nose, pouts her lips in a way that the mirror has proved many times is cute.

"How come I've not seen you, errrrr, Stadd? That's right, yeah?"

"I'm so glad you took the time to remember me."

Copying his joke is worse than not being witty at all. But it's done now. What else to say? What else? The only thing that's on her mind is what she came here for. So out it pops.

"How come you stopped calling?"

"Oh fuck, I need to be more pissed than this before we have a deep and meaningful."

He gulps down half of his Guinness.

"Before I make a complete arse of myself, you're going to need your backside out too, Cait."

"Hmmmm." Cait looks down at her glass. Empty. Fuck.

He takes a deep breath, grows an inch as he straightens from his belly. The movement is so slow, a little unsteady. A bear stretching up on two legs.

"Are you still interested in me?"

These were the sort of words that Cait wasn't good at. Why doesn't she say what she really thinks? Because she can't. Just can't. The silence grows too long.

"Your silence answers your own question, Cait. I'm not interested in getting fucked around."

No, no. Where were the words she needed?

Just do the kissing.

She reaches up and there is his mouth again. He parts

his lips to her and she slips her tongue over his. That earthy taste, yes, the cedar scent of his rough cheeks. She presses the hard bones of her hips against his thighs. Her nipples tighten.

Stadd pulls away, rubbing the back of his head.

"A yes or no would have done."

"You know my actions speak louder than words."

Shit, literally the worst thing she could say. Like an open and signed confession.

"Yeah, well after I came back to yours, you were kind of cold. And I started to think about how I always, shit," he takes another gulp from his glass. "How I always call you, come to see you."

"I'm here now, aren't I?"

He reaches for her hip, squeezes.

"So, do you want another drink?"

And before she can answer she sees the hand, hears the thump on Stadd's back.

"About time, you tight cunt."

"Might have known you'd have turned up at the opening of a wallet. I wasn't talking to your piss-ugly mug, Rik, you can get your own."

Rik's hair's been cut so he's not looking out with that Princess Di slant from under his fringe. His skin is all shiny and tight across his face. He's looking straight at her, like he's just been served tequila. Down in one. Cait's pretty sure that the opening of a wallet isn't why he was summoned. He looks awkward between her and Stadd, though. He's carrying his whole body like an accidental boner. Not wanting to make the choice between following Stadd to the bar like a puppy or being alone with Rik, Cait excuses herself for the bog.

Diggy's coming out of the gents as she's walking down the steps. His skin looks too pink against his lemon-checked Benny shirt. She hasn't a clue whether she should acknowledge him, so it's a relief when he starts up the conversation. Until it registers what he's saying.

"I've got no time for going softly on this one, Cait."

He's reminding Cait of a *Fruit Salad* chew. Not a good look, but he's trying.

"Sorry? About what?"

He pauses, slowly exhales through puckered lips. Balloon face indeed.

Why can't anyone just get straight to it tonight?

"Stop fucking around my best mate."

Is Rik his best mate? Is it Stadd? Cait's got no words. Sometimes she wonders if she ever learnt to speak at all. Diggy picks it up again.

"I know what's happening between you and Rik. And Stadd might not know yet, but I'm definitely going to tell him if you try and get with him again."

Diggy looks away, juts out his jaw and leaves Cait standing in front of the bogs. As she pushes open the door, though, she notices Natalie, hair as frizzy as ever, standing at the bar with Stadd, and pauses. Stadd's hand lingers on Natalie's arm. It touches a still place in Cait's belly. The eye of the storm.

As she stumbles into the stall, Cait feels sick that there's something happening between Stadd and Natalie.

Dragging down her jeans she remembers how Natalie was hanging around that night in Snobs. Cait knows she's got no right to be annoyed at Stadd or feel sick. But she does. The stillness in her belly is starting to burn. She needs him to be steady. She's ready to rely on him.

What if his steadiness goes?

What if Stadd starts cheating on her with Natalie?

She bends over to pull up her waistband, feels her heartbeat move out of sync with the music, giddiness rushing to her head.

What if he already has?

Maybe Cait has misread Natalie. Not a prissy pants. Maybe she's all earthy and natural, grunting her way through afternoon sex. Cait wants to go up to Stadd. To claim him. To show Natalie where to fuck off. What can she do now?

She unbolts the door, avoiding the mirrors, stumbles out into the pub. The music's pounding louder now, the place is filling up. Diggy's going to tell Stadd. Should she tell him instead? Ha! Not likely. What would happen then?

Stadd's back in his spot, turns to raise a full pint at her which she guesses is hers. She knows Diggy is watching her but refuses to catch his eye. Does he know the whole story to tell? Probably not, but even part of the story is bad enough.

Rik's at the door to the beer garden, lighting up. He bows his head forward to smile at her, which looks ridiculous without his long fringe. Would Diggy risk his friendship with Rik by ratting on him? Yes, because Rik never gives a fuck about being seen as the dirtbag he is.

Cait starts to walk towards Stadd but her knees are

wobbly and everything flickers with red. She holds her hand flat against the bar. Why do men's fuck ups show their bloke power, but women's fuck ups just show their fuck ups? She needs to go outside.

One foot in front of the other, that's all she needs. A push in the back for anyone in her way. Her body is lurching forward. Just keep going. She'll have to get past Rik to get outside. He's smirking at her zombie moves.

"Had a bit too much already have you?"

She nods, moves past him and through the doorway. But on second thoughts, she's not going to see this night through on her own. She reaches back. First Rik pinches her arse and then he lets Cait take his hand and pull him outside.

March 2018

Did you know or didn't you? Does it matter now?

All day I've been writing, walking, writing. Just for this last note to you I've settled back on the beach. I take in huge lungfuls of damp air, sitting on the same rock with the torch at my feet, but it's not the night it was yesterday. Tonight the clouds hang as if to kiss the sea. There is no moon, no stars.

For twenty-three years, these memories were buried in me like a sleeping winter bulb. The dream of our kiss, of our rooted feet, was the change in weather to wake this all up, Stadd.

Writing this, I've felt the heartache over losing what I'd been numb to. But heartache is just heartache. It doesn't mean you were my destiny, or any of that shit. I think it shows that I can love now, I can feel, in a way I couldn't then. My heart, like your waistline, has come of age.

I needed to recall the young man, with his thick dark quiff, and his old Crombie coat. With his earnest face between his girlfriend's legs, a bear lapping water. Your sweet face. I am not my pen, with its shiny nib and the sure, even flow of its ink. My chest feels like crumbling earth and that dormant bulb of my memory has bolted new shoots that pierce my ribs.

Oh, Stadd, I did such bad things. You blessed me once. You were warm hands and a safe bed away from cold concrete. It's not so hard to bring a man back, to conjure him with longing and persuasion, to make a portrait of him with a cocky pen. But you owe me no more blessings. Not even to listen to my apology.

If I was going to cast a spell tonight, this cloudy night without moon or stars, I'd take my swaggering pen and turn it to a sword.

And with this sword I'd slice through the tendrils around my feet, hack through the thick roots curling from your soles. I wouldn't steal any more kisses which weren't mine to take.

But in that moment, what we needed to feel, we would feel.

And what we needed to heal, would heal.

And with all those cords cut between us you'd be free from my need to search for you, to find a truth about me inside you, where I never should have looked before searching inside my own chest first. Released, I would spin you back around, twenty years and ten thousand miles. And you'd whirl back to where you've been all along.

And why would I want to cast this spell?

To let you go, Stadd.

To let you and the story go.

Author Biography

Claire HM is a fiction writer, poet and teacher based in (and writing about) her home city of Birmingham. In 2018 she had an essay published in the anthology, *I Wrote it Anyway*, about her experience of accessing university and the long journey of finding the confidence to write as a woman in her forties from a working-class background. Her work is now published in a growing number of literary publications, including *Tears in the Fence*, *Magma*, *The Rialto*, *streetcake*, *Coven Journal* and in *Cape Magazine*.

She most likes to write about identity within 'othered' perspectives, desire and consent, reclamation of femmes and sorceresses from Classical texts, and the politics and privilege of class and language. Most of all, she delights in exploring taboo subjects.

Claire channels her creativity through writing as an act of healing, and as an invitation for others to create the stories they need to access healing too. For details of how to work with Claire, visit https://clairehm.com/work-with-claire/

Social Media
@clairehmwriter
(Twitter, Instagram
and Facebook)

Enjoy the rest of our 2021 Shorts Season:

Pigskin by David Hartley

Something strange is happening to the animals on the farm.

A pig becomes bacon, chickens grow breadcrumbs, a cow turns to leather, a goat excretes cheese. As food becomes scarce and the looming 'pot-bellies' threaten to invade the safety of the sty, Pig knows he must get to the bottom of this strange phenomenon or face imminent death. Reminiscent of Animal Farm and darkly satirical, David Hartley interrogates the ethics of farming and the potential problems of genetic engineering, asking important questions about our relationship to the food – or animals – we eat.

"Pigskin is a knife-sharp, knowing fable about animal instincts and human ingenuity. David Hartley has a gift for creating stories that leave scars."

- Aliya Whiteley, author of The Loosening Skin

PowerPoint Eulogy by Mark Wilson

Three corporate hours have been allotted to commemorate the life of enigma, Bill Motluck. Employee memories of his life are crudely recounted onto a dusty projector. No one has ever been quite sure of his purpose. No one is quite sure who wrote the PowerPoint...but it seems to be exposing them all, one by one.

"In his wildly imaginative chapbook, PowerPoint Eulogy, Chicago writer and visual artist Mark Wilson paints a picture of corporate culture—and humanity at large—that is both soul-crushingly bleak and hilariously demented. Divided into forty-four presentation

"slides", the story centers on the memories a group of unnamed employees have of their recently deceased co-worker, Bill Motluck—a man so bland he enjoyed small talk about skim milk, and so desperate to fit in he once rented a newborn for Bring Your Kid to Work Day. Should we give in to the impulse to laugh at poor Bill, or feel sympathy for his plight? As the stories and little revelations pile up, it becomes harder and harder to decide—and the tension this creates is what ultimately makes this one-of-a-kind collection so impossible to put down. I laughed, I winced, I loved it".

- Mark Rader, Author of 'The Wanting Life'.

Muscle and Mouth by Louise Finnigan

"A beautifully written and compelling story"

- Kerry Hudson, Award-Winning Author of 'Lowborn'

"Muscle and Mouth made me feel the fracture of my own northern identity deep in my gut. It made me ache for home. It reminded me that leaving a place means giving pieces of yourself away; your rawness, your language and a certain kind of love. Louise Finnigan is a writer to watch."

- Jessica Andews, Author of 'Saltwater' and Winner of 2020 Portico Prize

Jade is prepping an A-Level assignment, all her sights set on Durham University. She's told she has to 'prove herself' and keep her away from the unsavoury types she calls her best friends. Yet Jade is reluctant to shun her corner of Manchester, where she finds the land rich, 'dark with energy'.

Hassan's Zoo by Ruth Brandt

Hassan's Zoo

When American soldiers invade Iraq searching for weapons of mass destruction, Kesari the Bengal tiger and other wildlife are at the mercy of guns and keeper, Hassan.

Entrenched in perpetual fear, Hassan must exercise Godly powers over his creatures in his attempts to save them - and himself.

A Village in Winter

"Mrs Gregory said to leave Frizz and his mum be for a while. Stop pestering. That poor woman with that lad."

In the chill of winter, the villagers play by the river, their play as harsh as the ice.

The Guts of a Mackerel by Clare Reddaway

"Who's Bobby Sands?" she asked, as she laid the fish on the face of a smiling young man with long wavy hair. "And what's a hunger strike?"

On a family holiday to her dad's Irish homeland, Eve's concerns about impressing local boy Liam are confronted by the stark reality of political and personal divisions during the Troubles. Former friends have turned into enemies, and this country of childhood memory is suddenly a lot less welcoming.

About Fly on the Wall Press

A publisher with a conscience. Publishing high quality anthologies on pressing issues, chapbooks and poetry products, from exceptional poets around the globe. Founded in 2018 by founding editor, Isabelle Kenyon.

Other publications:

Please Hear What I'm Not Saying (February 2018. Anthology, profits to Mind.)

Persona Non Grata (October 2018. Anthology, profits to Shelter and Crisis Aid UK.)

Bad Mommy / Stay Mommy by Elisabeth Horan
(May 2019. Chapbook.)

The Woman With An Owl Tattoo by Anne Walsh Donnelly
(May 2019. Chapbook.)

the sea refuses no river by Bethany Rivers
(June 2019. Chapbook.)

White Light White Peak by Simon Corble
(July 2019. Artist's Book.)

Second Life by Karl Tearney
(July 2019. Full collection)

The Dogs of Humanity by Colin Dardis
(August 2019. Chapbook.)

Small Press Publishing: The Dos and Don'ts by Isabelle Kenyon
(January 2020. Non-Fiction.)

Alcoholic Betty by Elisabeth Horan
(February 2020. Chapbook.)

Awakening by Sam Love
(March 2020. Chapbook.)

Grenade Genie by Tom McColl
(April 2020. Full Collection.)

House of Weeds by Amy Kean and Jack Wallington
(May 2020. Full Collection.)
No Home In This World by Kevin Crowe
(June 2020. Short Stories.)
How To Make Curry Goat by Louise McStravick
(July 2020. Full Collection.)
The Goddess of Macau by Graeme Hall
(August 2020. Short Stories.)
The Prettyboys of Gangster Town by Martin Grey
(September 2020. Chapbook.)
The Sound of the Earth Singing to Herself by Ricky Ray
(October 2020. Chapbook.)
Mancunian Ways (Anthology of poetry and photography)
Inherent by Lucia Orellana Damacela
(November 2020. Chapbook.)
Medusa Retold by Sarah Wallis
(December 2020. Chapbook.)
We Are All Somebody compiled by Samantha Richards (February
2021. Anthology. Profits to Street Child United.)
Pigskin by David Hartley
(February 2021. Shorts.)
Aftereffects by Jiye Lee
(March 2021. Chapbook.)
Someone Is Missing Me by Tina Tamsho-Thomas
(March 2021. Full Collection.)
PowerPoint Eulogy by Mark Wilson
(April 2021. Shorts)

Social Media:
@fly_press (Twitter)
@flyonthewall_poetry (Instagram)
@flyonthewallpress (Facebook)